KELEV'S
JOURNEY

KELEV'S JOURNEY

A Jewish Dog Wanders Home

David Hammerstein

Illustrations by Ed Shems

Wyndebirk Books
Pittsburgh, PA

Editor: Stephanie Golden
Designer: Judith Arisman

ISBN: 978-0-9973416-0-7
LCCN: 2016903273

davidhammersteinauthor.com

Wyndebirk Books
Pittsburgh, PA

Contents

1

···

A Dog Yearns for Yiddishkeit

Kelev, a lively black Labrador retriever, lived with his guardians, Mordecai and Esther Metzger, and their seven children in Pittsburgh's Squirrel Hill neighborhood. Kelev sported a shiny, coal-black coat that matched the black garments worn by his guardians. One spring day, Kelev began his journey as a Jew.

The Metzgers and their children showered him with affection. The children cuddled and kissed him before they went to bed. Mrs. Metzger often told Kelev that her heart overflowed with joy when she saw him. Mr. Metzger constantly praised his loyalty and compas-

sion. He slept on a bed filled with goose down, and the Metzgers served him select cuts of beef brisket.

But the Metzgers also imposed restrictions—no pork, no car rides on the Sabbath, no meals without washing his paws—and Kelev felt deprived. What was more, he felt a spiritual void. Something was missing in his life, but he could not put his paw on it.

Having just turned one year old, Kelev was allowed to roam around the Metzgers' yard. Schmalzie, the neighbors' beagle, often came over to talk.

One day Kelev was bemoaning his plight: "I have no freedom. Too many rules and regulations!"

Schmalzie barked, "You have religious obligations to uphold."

"Why do I have these obligations?" Kelev asked.

"Because you are Jewish," Schmalzie growled.

"What's Jewish?"

"It's a behavioral disorder that makes you feel guilty," Schmalzie whined, as tears welled up.

"Is that why I feel bad when my guardians tell me how tired they are when they take me out at night?"

"You're talking like a real Yid."

"So, tell me more about my Jewish obligations."

"Judaism imposes 613 obligations, known in Hebrew as mitzvot."

"What are some of them?"

"Know G-d as One, love G-d, study Torah, bind tefillin on the foreleg, don't seek revenge, don't bear a grudge, and be kind to widows and orphans. The list goes on."

"It must be a mighty challenge to perform all 613!"

"Ah, for you, Mr. Kelev, we'll make it an even 600 and call it a day."

"Why do Jews bear these obligations?"

"G-d says so," Schmalzie growled. "Am I going to argue with G-d? And besides, these obligations sustain a long tradition of following our forbearers' paw steps," he said.

"So, G-d chose the Jews to perform the mitzvot. Is that why my guardians call Jews the Chosen People?"

"Yes, but you and I are not people."

"Then, we are the Chosen Pack," Kelev said.

"You are already talking like a yeshiva bocher," Schmalzie chuckled. He taught Kelev several more mitzvot, and then they both went home.

His talk with Schmalzie helped Kelev dig up his Jewish roots. Reflecting on their conversation, he realized that this new awareness of Judaism was beginning to fill his spiritual void. The notion to become a rabbi entered his mind. He assumed he was likely a canine Kohen because he lived with an orthodox Jewish family—and he already had a full-length black coat. As a rabbi, Kelev thought, he would seek out and counsel other Jewish dogs in the neighborhood. Many dogs were uncertain about their lineage, and he would help Jewish dogs sniff it out.

During walks with Mr. and Mrs. Metzger in the town's shopping district, Kelev had observed how certain members of the Chabad-Lubavitch movement approached pedestrians who they thought might be Jewish. They typically asked, "Are you Jewish?" If the pedestrian said "yes," the Hasidic Jew performed a ritual, such as a prayer, with the person.

The following day, Kelev was patrolling his yard, looking for souls to save. An English springer spaniel passed by and watered the Metzgers' bushes. Kelev decided to try out his new shtick.

"Excuse me. Are you Jewish?" he asked.

"My name is Roderick," the spaniel replied. "I'm from a distinguished English family. Can't you tell?"

"There are Jews in England," Kelev said.

Roderick paused. "I believe I have a maternal great-grandmother named Rebecca. Her original name might have been Rivkah. Perhaps I do have Jewish lineage."

"Any dog that can relieve himself on a stranger's yard with such impunity must have acquired chutzpah from somewhere," Kelev remarked.

"I'm keeping your bushes green," Roderick barked back. "And I don't charge extra for the favor."

"Oy veh," Kelev moaned. "Let me teach you some manners. Better yet, I'll teach you a mitzvah."

"What's that?" Roderick asked.

"It's an obligation from G-d," Kelev beamed, proudly showing off his newly acquired knowledge. Kelev retrieved a blue and white towel from a lawn chair and draped it over Roderick like a tallis. He recited a Hebrew blessing to celebrate the awakening of Roderick's Jewish identity, and Roderick repeated it. Kelev and Roderick celebrated their new friendship with a Kiddush using doggy treats that Kelev retrieved from his porch. Roderick then scampered back home as it was time for lunch.

Elated by his new role as spiritual adviser for the kosher canine corps, Kelev reflected on the challenge Rabbi Hillel had posed in ancient times: "If I am not for others, what am I?" So many souls to save! Much work lay ahead. But now, Kelev was exhausted and slouched back to his porch for an afternoon nap. Napping didn't provoke guilt. Kelev was preparing for his next spiel.

2

···

The Bible, 5776 Edition?

Every evening, while Mrs. Metzger read Bible stories to her seven children, Kelev sprawled across the living room floor to listen. One evening she asked, "What lessons do we learn from these stories?"

Adam, the oldest child, responded, "The Biblical characters display their vision and their courage in their devotion to G-d."

Miriam, the youngest, said that the stories inspired her to think about Kelev because of his overwhelming devotion to the family. In her eyes, Kelev was a hero.

"Mama, will G-d change the Bible to include stories about Kelev?" she asked.

This question stunned Mrs. Metzger. She had never considered the possibility that G-d might revise the Torah. G-d had expressed his love for his children with the Torah, his greatest gift to humankind. He gave the Jewish people the Torah as is. "Mimi, that's a deeply profound question," Mrs. Metzger told her daughter. "Let me ponder it."

Meanwhile, Kelev's ears perked up. The prospect of a Bible passage about his heroics intrigued him and he searched his memory for examples of his courage and vision; he came up with some pretty impressive examples.

Kelev Maccabee. During a recent shopping trip, Mr. Metzger had brought home a twenty-five–pound bag of dog food. The thought of one single bag of food worried Kelev. What if it ran out before Mr. Metzger could replenish it? So he prayed for additional bags of food. The next day, searching the kitchen pantry, he stumbled across eight of them! His prayer had inspired a miracle.

Beyond the Lions' Den. In Biblical times, when Daniel walked into a lions' den, G-d sent an angel to close the lions' mouths to save Daniel. A week earlier, Kelev had committed an even more dangerous act. At the home of his neighbor, Kefira the cat, he waded into a herd of quarreling kittens—Kefira's visiting nieces and nephews—and calmed them down by tossing them rubber balls to distract them. His act was not only courageous, but needed no divine intervention.

Modern-Day Moses. The dogs in Squirrel Hill often romped in nearby Frick Park to let off steam. On some days, so many dogs flocked to the park, that it became congested. Noticing a somber Doberman pinscher named Shlimazl eyeing the scene, Kelev smelled a rat.

One day, Shlimazl braced himself in front of the park entrance, blocking all dogs other than fellow Dobermans from entering. Kelev confronted him. "So what gives you the right to be the big macher here?"

"I'm just exercising our breed's territorial claims."

"All dogs consider this park our land of milk and honey."

"Sorry, hintl. If you want milk, chase a cow. If you seek honey, dive into a beehive."

"You'll be hearing from me!"

Kelev had made this threat on the spur of the moment. Now he needed a plan. His brain swung into action, and he visited his beagle neighbor, Schmalzie. "Hey, Schmalz. I need your help."

"What's up?"

"Shlimazl and his minions have taken over Frick Park. We need to dislodge them."

"Such chutzpah!"

Kelev and Schmalzie wandered into the garage, seeking ideas for liberating the park. Kelev spotted a frog costume that a child had worn in a Purim carnival. "Jump into this," he ordered Schmalzie. "We'll show that phony pharaoh a plague or two."

Kelev and Schmalzie scampered over to the Park entrance. They stopped in front of Shlimazl and stared at him.

"Who's this giant, green reptile?" asked Shlimazl.

"His name is Tzfardeha. I have assembled a teeming army of these frogs. They're waiting around the corner. Unless you relent, I'll order them to storm the Park!"

Shlimazl quickly backed away from the entrance. "Come and go as you please. I'm out of here."

Kelev and Schmalzie entered the park to check that an exodus was really happening. They witnessed a flood of Dobermans streaming out of the rear exit.

"I'm green, but not mean," Schmalzie chuckled. "Those dogs are lucky we spared them from beasts, hail, and locusts."

Several weeks after Miriam had first asked her question, she wanted to know again whether G-d would

revise the Bible. "Mimi, the matter is in G-d's hands," said her mother.

Kelev, however, continued to feel confident that G-d would revise the Bible to include stories about him: *So many opportunities to enrich the Bible,* he thought. *G-d, with infinite wisdom, will select the appropriate tales.* Meanwhile, he had a lot to think about. Would he go on a book-signing tour for the new Bible edition? Make the rounds of TV talk shows? Kelev marveled at his many virtues—the most notable being humility.

3

...

The Vanishing Brisket

Mrs. Metzger was famous for her delicious beef briskets. Some went so far as to say that her briskets were truly heavenly. One Friday afternoon, she roasted a brisket for the family's Sabbath dinner. When it was done, she left it on her kitchen table while she fetched a tablecloth. Kelev was resting on the kitchen floor, but Mrs. Metzger trusted Kelev, a dog with a heart of gold.

When she returned to the kitchen, the brisket had vanished. Mrs. Metzger stared at the empty platter. "My-brisket, my baby! What happened?" she shrieked.

Slowly, Kelev lifted his head. He peered at Mrs. Metzger with sullen eyes, sunken jowls, and limp ears. Defiantly he pointed his nose toward the tablet of the Ten Commandments on the wall. Mrs. Metzger glanced at it, and her eye fell on Commandment Nine, "Thou shalt not bear false witness against thy neighbor." She burst into tears, ashamed of having even considered the possibility that Kelev had devoured the brisket.

But how did the brisket vanish? Mrs. Metzger wondered. Did it grow wings and fly away? Did a stray animal invade the house and eat it? The doors and windows showed no signs of an intruder. The mystery vexed her.

Then she had a revelation. G-d had sent an angel to retrieve the brisket for the Sabbath dinner he was hosting for the angels. What a mitzvah that Mrs. Metzger could contribute to such a celebration! Her excitement was so great that she told Kelev about this divination. He jumped up, wagged his tail, and barked. His eyes now gleamed. What a way to usher in the Sabbath!

"I must share the story of this miracle with the rabbi! I'll be back soon," she told Kelev, and she ran out of the house with the empty platter.

Kelev marveled at Mrs. Metzger's keen insights, but then he suddenly felt tired. He told himself that all this excitement had exhausted him; surely it couldn't be a meal that had made him sleepy. So he flopped back on the kitchen floor for a nap. He felt good—especially since he had a premonition that angels would be calling on Mrs. Metzger the next time she made another of her specialties—succulent roast lamb.

4

...

The Mighty Mediator

Kelev used his newly found freedom to guard the Metzgers' home like a hawk. He policed the yard daily, chasing away squirrels and butterflies. A sense of calm pervaded the place. Yet Kelev felt his guardians didn't appreciate the heavy burden he bore: when he slept, he kept one eye open to spot intruders. Well ... usually one eye was open.

Lately, Kelev had been worrying about an invasion of migrant squirrels. He fretted that these intruders from surrounding counties were bringing in new strains of

acorns. The local squirrels were going nuts over these foreign acorns, and he was concerned about possible skir-
mishes. Duty beckoned, so Kelev swung into action.

Stepping outside to nose around, he spotted his
neighbor, Schmalzie.

"Hey, Schmalz. Over here," Kelev barked.

Schmalzie scampered over to the Metzgers' lawn.
"Reporting for duty, Captain Kelev!"

Kelev pointed to a mound of acorns in his yard.
"Look at these, Schmalz. How do we check them out?"

"Let's summon Sammy the squirrel. He's our
friend," Schmalzie suggested.

Schmalzie and Kelev spotted Sammy in his usual

digs, near a towering oak tree. Sammy sniffed the acorns, then nibbled a few.

"A strong, smoky aroma and a rich nutty flavor. Clearly not a local variety."

"That's what worries me," said Kelev. "I've seen foreign squirrels dart into our neighborhood. They sport darker gray coats and bushier tails than Pittsburgh squirrels. They're bringing in this contraband."

"We must assert our territorial rights," Schmalzie growled.

"Let's first try diplomacy," Kelev said. "Perhaps I can strike a deal."

"Kind of like, 'You are a dog and a diplomat.'"

"You got it, Schmalz," Kelev said.

Sammy chimed in, "I'll try it."

The next day, Kelev convened a council comprised of himself, Schmalzie, and three squirrels—Sammy and two intruders.

Kelev opened the proceedings. "We have witnessed the invasion of migrant squirrels. We have shown restraint. But our patience has limits. We cannot tolerate an assault on our territorial integrity."

A foreign squirrel responded, "We appreciate the opportunity to present our case. I am glad you raise the issue of territorial integrity. Our ancestors once roamed the woods of Squirrel Hill. Over 250 years ago, following the founding of Pittsburgh, settlers drove our ancestors from our homes. We have sought refuge in surrounding counties. We live in a Diaspora but still yearn for our ancestral homeland."

Realizing they had prejudged the wandering squirrels, Kelev and Schmalzie felt tears come to their eyes.

"Every year during our Seder," the vagrant continued, "we recite a prayer: 'Next Year in Shady Avenue.'"

Kelev now sobbed. He no longer viewed the foreign squirrels as aggressors; rather they were uprooted refugees seeking a connection with their homeland. "We open our homes and hearts to pilgrims," he cried.

"I speak for my compatriots," one of the intruding squirrels responded. "We appreciate your gracious acceptance. We look forward to future visits and acorn exchanges." The dogs and squirrels concluded their conference with a feast: the squirrels munched acorns while Kelev and Schmalzie chomped doggy treats.

Schmalzie dashed back to play ball with the kids in his home, and Kelev sat down in his yard to reflect on how he had secured the peace and made new friends. He gushed with joy about his new role as peacemaker. He had pursued Jewish values by settling a dispute with principles and reason, not through force or conflict. His accomplishments, though, exhausted him, so he returned to his house and flopped down on the floor to nap. His snores echoed. Both eyes were closed.

5

···

Big Bad Borscht

Despite his occasional grumbling, Kelev enjoyed his life. He was adjusting to the daily responsibilities of his mitzvot. He savored the affection of his guardians and their children and the tranquility of his neighborhood. But one day, a bossy bulldog named Borscht barged into Squirrel Hill with his guardians, Ivan and Galina Moscowitz. Borscht flaunted his Russian heritage. He was proud that on a hot day, he could drink any dog under the table. Borscht could down five bowls of water without taking a potty break. Few dogs could boast of such stamina.

Borscht decided to introduce himself to the other dogs in the neighborhood and lay down the law—starting with Kelev. He had heard stories about Kelev's popularity and wanted to size him up. Having grown up in a tough neighborhood, Borchst had little patience for courtesy and diplomacy, and strutted up the street, thrusting his chest out and cocking his head high. Then he stormed onto Kelev's lawn and marched right up to him. Borscht pressed his nose against Kelev's nose and stared into Kelev's eyes.

"So, you're the terrible takef in this neighborhood," Borscht bellowed.

This bravado startled Kelev, but he kept his cool. "I'm just one of the guys," he said calmly.

"Look, buster, I'm the new boss around here. All major decisions in the doggy domain go through me."

Schmalzie, the beagle, ran over to witness this encounter. "What gives?"

"We have a new kid on the block. He's giving us a lesson in civics."

"Whoa," Schmalzie said. "We have a czar now in Pittsburgh?"

"Look, you little schnitzel," Borscht growled. "I'm in control. No harassing the mail carrier without my permission. No backyard digging unless I say so. No barking at night. No venturing out at night except for potty breaks. And remember my favorite word—'nyet.'"

Kelev and Schmalzie looked stunned. Inwardly, they were snickering. To them, Borscht seemed all bark and no bite, but they suppressed their laughter.

"I need to finish making my rounds," Borscht said, as he shook his tail and trotted up the street.

Schmalzie looked up at Kelev. "He sure is full of spit and vinegar."

"We'll make a softy out of him," Kelev reassured him. "If we tell Borscht to fall in line, he'll resist. But if something makes him realize he needs to change his ways, he'll reform all on his own. Let's give him some time."

Borscht stayed away from Kelev for several days. Word was that he was bullying other dogs in the neighborhood, but with little success.

One day, Borscht showed up on Kelev's lawn, looking a bit more subdued and conciliatory than before.

"Hey, Kelev. You know I'm still the boss."

"Of course." Kelev was keeping to his policy of no confrontation. He wanted Borscht to change from within.

"I need your advice."

"I'm all ears."

"You know that auburn spaniel on the cul-de-sac? Her radiant gold coat, soft brown eyes, and dainty paws captivate me."

"Schmoozie. A Jewish American puppy."

"That's her. Well, um … is she … well, is she … is she …?"

"Is she attached?"

"Yes, that's what I meant."

"I'd say she's available—to the right doggy," Kelev said, and winked.

"Perhaps you could introduce us."

"I'm not a yenta. Remember, you're the big boss. You make things happen."

Looking away, head drooping, Borscht murmured, "How can I attract her?"

"The alpha male dogs melt when they see Schmoozie. But the dogs she actually likes are calm and sensitive, in touch with their inner feelings."

Borscht looked perplexed. "I'm going home now. I need time to reflect."

Several days later, Schmalzie and Kelev were kibitzing in Kelev's yard. Borscht meandered up and, with a sheepish smile, said, "Hi Kelev. Hi Schmalzie. How are you fellows? Great to see you."

"We've been thinking about your curfew," Schmalzie piped.

"Oh, don't worry about curfews," Borscht said, smiling broadly.

"What have you been up to?" Kelev asked.

"I've gotten in touch with my inner self. When I looked inward, I saw a heart of steel and a stormy soul, and I realized I didn't want to live like that anymore. I want to nurture love within me. I want to share my love. So I'm learning to connect to my inner puppy. I spend my mornings marveling at sunrises. During the day, I admire the autumn foliage. In the evening, I gaze at sunsets," Borscht sighed.

"I'm touched. And I'm kwelling," Kelev said.

"Okay, got to go now," Borscht said abruptly. "I'll see you fellows later."

As Borscht turned to leave, Kelev asked if he was headed toward the cul-de-sac.

"Oh … in that general direction," Borscht replied.

As Borscht swaggered up the street, he sang a ballad about his Squirrel Hill sweetheart.

"From a Siberian snowstorm to a tropical breeze," Kelev beamed.

6

...

Cousin Kwetchie

Kelev's cousin Kwetchie could talk up a storm. She moped and whined and saw the dark sides of clouds. When she wasn't relieving herself, she rained on other dogs' parades. Yet Kwetchie, a yellow Lab, claimed she represented the sunny side of the family and maintained that Kelev, as a black Lab, lurked on the dark side. Kelev just chuckled at this. He and Kwetchie weren't "kissing cousins," but they got along. Their mothers were littermates. Kwetchie's guardians, Mr. and Mrs. Dunkelwolke, visited the Metzgers often so that Kwetchie and Kelev could see each other.

In Kelev's opinion, Kwetchie's most prominent trait was her generosity. Did she deserve a donor's plaque in the doggy shul? Not exactly. What Kwetchie dished out so graciously was advice, opinions, and demands. For example, on a recent visit, Kwetchie barked out a series of orders.

"Straighten up the blanket on the back porch and clean off the leaves. Don't drink out of my water bowl! I don't like the way you slobber when you drink."

Kwetchie then elaborated on her health and beauty concerns. "I need to visit the vet and get my nails filed. I want a bubble bath to bring out the gold shimmer in my coat. And I'm thinking of getting a tummy tuck. The years are starting to show. Oy, do I have tsoris. It never stops."

"OK, enough already," Kelev said. "Let's move on."

So Kwetchie told him about the new direction her life was taking, reminding him that Labrador retrievers had a therapeutic tradition as seeing-eye dogs and companions for people with emotional disorders. She informed Kelev that she had recently become a therapist, counseling other dogs.

"Well, you're not shy about dispensing advice," Kelev said.

"I deal with a lot of issues: interbreed marriages, objections to leash laws, conditions at dog boarders, veterinarian care reform (under the Affordable Dog Care Act), and issues with commercial dog walkers," Kwetchie responded.

"You must have some interesting patients."

"A Dalmatian told me he's developed a closer relationship with his dog walker than his guardian. He seeks a divorce. A dachshund wants to marry a German shepherd. Their friends say they are incompatible, but they think their mutual German heritage will bind them together. A boxer complained that the attendants in the dog-boarding place are insensitive, but they act nice in front of his guardians. He's got some real anger-management issues."

"Tell me more," Kelev said.

"I have to put up with a lot," Kwetchie said. "One

dog told me I'm as tart as pickled herring. I told him he's as exciting as gefilte fish."

Afterward, Kelev thought about this conversation. Should he seek therapy? Engrossed in deep reflection, he fell asleep. In a dream, he found himself in Kwetchie's therapy office, where her diplomas and professional certificates adorned the walls. He lay on a reclining chair while Kwetchie, sitting on an office chair, sprang into action.

"Kelev, you're too passive. You lie on the floor nearly all day and snooze your life away. You let other dogs walk all over you. I heard that a Russian bulldog bullied you silly. You burden your guardians, whimpering to go out for potty breaks late at night. You turn your nose up at conventional dog food, insisting on select cuts of brisket."

These allegations jarred Kelev awake. He jumped up onto all four legs, blinked, and shook himself. Then he thought over Kwetchie's accusations. Lazy? Passive? No! He was reflective, deliberate, and calm. He was a leader. He had introduced other dogs to Judaism, mediated a peace agreement among the squirrels, subdued an aggressive bulldog, and liberated Frick Park from tyrant Dobermans. His friends sought his advice. A burden to his guardians? Absolutely not. His guardians praised him. Mimi Metzger thought G-d should revise the Bible to record his heroics. If Kelev were not a dog, he would be a real mensch. "I don't need therapy!" he said to himself.

Kelev concluded that he must challenge Kwetchie and set the record straight. She was not qualified to be a psychotherapist—she was a quack. But he decided to wait before confronting her. This latest outrage had tired him out. Time for another nap.

7

...

Kelev and Kefira Dart into Danger

Kelev was relaxing on his back porch when Kefira, his striped, amber cat neighbor, tiptoed across his lawn. "Hey, Kelev," she called, "I have an idea for an adventure."

"Not interested," Kelev snarled. "You know I'm not speaking to you."

"Aw, Kelev, you're not holding a grudge, are you?"

"I'm angry and I'm not going to take it anymore!"

What had upset the normally unflappable Kelev? The previous week, Kefira had played a trick on him. She

snatched his rubber ducky and ran away with it; Kelev naturally went after her. The Metzgers saw this pursuit, but Kefira managed to drop the rubber ducky on the sly, so Kelev seemed to be chasing her without provocation. Mrs. Metzger came out to scold him. "Shame on you, Kelev—chasing an innocent little cat! No doggy treats for a week."

Poor Kelev, banished to the doghouse, so to speak. He had been mighty mad, and he was still seething.

"Kelev, it was a joke. I want to make up for it. Now, listen to my idea," Kefira pleaded.

Kelev was all heart and good nature prevailed, so he couldn't say no.

Kefira spun her plan: to walk across a cable of Pittsburgh's South Tenth Street Bridge, the longest bridge spanning the Monongahela River. She painted a picture of how the duo would mesmerize drivers: two adversaries, a dog and a cat, collaborating in a high-wire stunt! The stakes were high. If they made it across the bridge, the rewards would be major. Pet food companies would offer endorsements, showering Kefira and Kelev with cash and fame.

"So, what do you think?" Kefira asked.

"Not my cup of tea," Kelev replied.

"Come on, Kelev," Kefira said. "You're not scared, are you? I'm the one who's supposed to be the scaredy-cat."

"Let me think about it," Kelev said. He flopped down on his porch and sank into deep thought.

Kefira went home to give Kelev time to think about her proposal. She returned an hour later.

"So what gives, Kelev?"

Kelev had concluded that he couldn't refuse Kefira's challenge. What would the other dogs in the neighborhood think—since Kefira was sure to spread the word that he was chicken? He bounced up. "I'm in. Let's do it."

Kelev and Kefira headed toward the bridge, giggling as they talked about their impending fame.

They arrived at the bridge just as rush hour began. Traffic was building. The only suspension bridge in Pittsburgh—1,275 feet long and rising to fifty feet above the water—it was supported by two thirteen-inch cables. The bridge's length and height stunned Kelev and Kefira, and the narrowness of the cable gave them pause.

"You sure you want to go ahead with this?' Kelev asked.

"Of course," Kefira replied, as her legs trembled. "You go first."

Kelev climbed onto one of the suspension cables and walked about fifty feet. He looked back to check on Kefira and saw that she had climbed onto the cable from the road, where it was only a foot above the ground, but

she had frozen. "I can't do it," she screamed. "I'm scared."
Her timidity baffled Kelev. Cats climbed trees and util-
ity poles. Yet here was Kefira, really being a scaredy-cat.
Kelev continued on; he had to protect his reputation. But
now he was on his own.

As he moved higher along the cable, he also got
scared. After about 100 feet, he too froze in fear. Meanwhile the bridge traffic had ground to a halt as drivers
peered up at him. He heard the whirring of a rescue he-
licopter approaching from behind. But seeing it only
frightened him more. His muscles stiffened; his paws lost
their grip; and he fell. He plunged toward the river, then

felt his snout hit the water. His eyes snapped open—to see Kefira spraying him with his rubber ducky.

Kelev jumped up. "What happened?" he asked. "Who rescued me from the river?"

"What river?" Kefira asked. "You fell asleep on your porch. I woke you up with a shower."

"Oh, what a relief!" Kelev gasped. "Saved from certain death and being eaten by river rats!"

"So, what about our adventure?" Kefira asked.

"Let's just go to the pond in the park with rubber ducky. We'll round up some ducks and geese for a game of Duck Duck Goose."

8

...

A Dog Debate

Kelev loved to stick his nose into an argument. But one Friday evening, he sat on the sidelines while his guardians and their neighbors tangled in a dog debate. The Metzgers were hosting Sabbath dinner for neighbors—the Liebs, the guardians of Schmoozie, the beautiful spaniel Borscht was courting; and Borscht's guardians, the Moscowitz family. Schmoozie and Borscht had come along.

In the middle of the dinner conversation, Mrs. Metzger suddenly asked, "Who's the best dog in the neighborhood?" This question broke the peace of the Shabbos; boasts and tirades flew through the air. The three dogs sought cover under the dining room table while the humans harangued each other. "We'll stay under the table, but keep above the fray," Schmoozie whispered to Kelev and Borchst.

Mr. Lieb fired the first shot in the skirmish. "Let me tell you how compassionate Schmoozie is. One day, a skunk showed up in our yard and confronted her, saying, 'No wisecracks, doggy. I can pollute the air worse than the belching steel mills during the depths of Pittsburgh's smog era.' Schmoozie answered, 'I understand your powers, but I know you prefer to go green and protect our planet. I judge you with my heart, not with my nose, and I can tell that you are sensitive and caring.' Tears welled

up in the skunk's eyes. He plucked roses from the neighbor's garden and gave Schmoozie a bouquet. Schmoozie said, 'Sweet. I'll remember you by this.'"

This speech made Schmoozie giggle. She placed her paw on Borchst's paw and whispered, "See how kind I am!" Borchst sighed.

Mr. Moscowitz spoke up. "So, Schmoozie's a brownnose. Borscht is the best! He has the soul of Tolstoy and the heart of Tchaikovsky."

Under the table, Borchst grinned.

"Borscht is a bust," Mr. Lieb sneered. "He has the personality of a rotten beet."

"Borscht has courage," Mr. Moscowitz countered. "One morning, a bear stormed into our yard and began to ravage the bushes. Borscht marched out to confront it: 'Hey, Teddy. Back to your Cub Scout den.' The bear retreated to the woods. He would not go up against a Bolshevik bulldog."

"Did that confrontation occur last week?' Mr. Lieb asked.

"Yes," Mr. Moscowitz replied.

"Let's get real," Mr. Lieb scoffed. "I saw it happen. That was no bear. It was a chipmunk."

"Well, it was a chipmunk with the ferocity of a bear," Mr. Moscowitz said.

Kelev and Schmoozie chuckled. Borchst grimaced.

Now Mr. Metzger entered the fray. "Kelev is so virtuous! Let me tell you a story of Biblical proportions. One day a huge snake slithered into our garden. It cracked a sly smile and said, 'Can I interest you in some shiny red

apples?' Kelev barked back, 'You're rotten to the core. Out, out, you slimy serpent!' The snake slipped away."

"Wow, Kelev," Schmoozie said. "It took courage to stand up to the sneaky snake!"

"I resisted the forbidden fruit, but I fear that the serpent might have returned to tempt Mrs. Metzger," Kelev said.

"Why?" Schmoozie asked.

Kelev pointed to the apple pie on Mrs. Metzger's dessert tray. And he began to worry. Would G-d banish Kelev and the Metzgers from their home in paradise? Not likely, Kelev reassured himself. So many good deeds were waiting to get done in Squirrel Hill. G-d needed Kelev, the mitzvot macher.

9

...

Kelev Goes to Gotham

Kelev loved New York City. He had resisted the temptation of the serpent's apple in Pittsburgh, but the Big Apple captured his heart. On a visit to the city with the Metzgers, he painted the town red.

Their first stop was the Statue of Liberty. Kelev imagined the flood of immigrants arriving in Ellis Island many decades ago, and thought about his journey as a Jew. Marveling at the Statue of Liberty, he wondered who this woman was. Mrs. Liberty? Probably her name was once Mrs. Lieberman, because she had greeted hordes of

immigrants from Eastern European shtetls from 1880 to 1920. Most likely she changed her name to Mrs. Liberty in a gesture to New York's diverse population. Kelev was moved by the statue's inscription, "Give me your tired, your poor, your huddled masses ...". But he couldn't understand why Mrs. Liberty thrust her torch upward. A more fitting gesture would have been for her to stoop down, filling a bowl with dog food.

Kelev wondered why so many Jews had fled Europe. It couldn't have been that the delis in New York

were better than those in Minsk, Lodz, and Warsaw. He
had heard Mr. and Mrs. Metzger talk about pogroms in
Eastern Europe, but he couldn't understand what had in-
cited violence against the Jews who only wanted to keep
G-d's covenant. Kelev thought it must have been diffi-
cult for the Jews to leave their homes and, in some cases,
their relatives. Could he leave home? He would even miss
cousin Kwetchie. The thought pained Kelev, but he imagined he could do so if it meant making Aliyah to Israel.

The next stop was Orchard Street on the Lower
East Side. Over one hundred years ago, Mr. and Mrs.
Metzger's forebears had worked as shopkeepers, tailors,
and seamstresses in this neighborhood. A tour guide de-
scribed the hardships of immigrants with large extended
families who lived in small, dark, cramped apartments
with poor sanitation and ventilation. Yet the families'
spiritual strength sustained them. They had hope for a
better life in America.

Thinking of his clean, spacious home in Squirrel
Hill with its large, shady lawn, Kelev saw how America
had bestowed peace and prosperity upon the Jews.

After a visit to the United Nations, the day ended
with a stroll in Central Park. Kelev noticed that other
dogs strutted along the path with more poise and dignity than he had seen among the diplomats. He re-

flected on his visit and on the pogroms that had driven Jews to America. Why did humans have the propensity to hate when dogs could live and let live? He decided to ponder that question another day and sought the shade of a large oak tree for an afternoon nap in the Park.

10

···

Kelev for President

Kelev cherished his role as G-d's mitzvah macher in Squirrel Hill, but sensed another calling: the down and dirty business of politics. Pittsburgh's city council had recently imposed restrictive leash laws and bans on barking between certain hours. It was up to him to stop such abuses of power. Kelev's inspiration to enter public service was the city's late mayor, Sophie Masloff. Mayor Masloff had been a real Yiddishe mama who would never restrict a dog's freedom. She sought dignity for dogs. Since her passing, no politician was pursuing canine rights. So Kelev had to take matters into his own paws. He thought of running for city council. But why stop there? Mayor? Governor? Senator? President? *President*, he thought. *Now, I'm starting to make some sense.*

But was the nation ready for a doggy president? Certainly dogs offered many virtues. They had pure hearts, while humans had demonstrated unlimited capacity for incompetence and cruelty. Kelev had learned something about the rough and tumble world of politics from the dog debate at the Metzgers' dinner table. While the humans had engaged in a virtual food fight over who was the best dog in the neighborhood, the dogs communed peacefully under the table.

Of course, Kelev planned to run a civil campaign. No rolling in the mud. No baiting his opponent with red-meat accusations. He would stick to meat-and-potatoes issues. As a kosher dog, he would naturally refrain from pork-barrel politics. Then, once he was elected, instead of a cabinet of boring bureaucrats, he would create a kitchen cabinet stocked with dogs who could sniff out the meat of weighty issues. There would be no secretary of state sticking his nose in other nations' affairs. Kelev would appoint a secretary of steak who bluntly asked, "What's your beef?" In a Kelev administration, with bulldog Borchst as national security advisor, the nation would play an active role as a "souper power." Kelev would run a squeaky-clean government. With Schmalzie as attorney general, no one would have a chance to grease the wheels for public officials. Kelev also needed a running mate. Who better than his neighbor Schmoozie? They could scamper around the spacious White House lawn.

So Kelev would uphold Mayor Masloff's legacy by focusing on kitchen-table issues. But the thought of these responsibilities was exhausting. He flopped down on his porch for an afternoon nap. As he drifted into slumber, he decided to delegate much of the work to his loyal lieutenants. Kelev thought of himself as a big-picture pooch. He would let others sweat the small stuff.

11

...

Kelev Fights Prejudice

Kelev was steaming. The chill of the December morning couldn't cool him off. Sprawled on the kitchen floor, he was hard at work planning to combat growing prejudice against certain species. In fact, he was placing his campaign for president on the back burner because these local injustices required his immediate attention. What most outraged him were ill-willed diatribes against dogs. An extremist political group, the Petless People Party, was charging that dogs were lazy. Lazy? They should see Kelev at work!

The Petless People Party's slogan was "Homes are just for humans." The party was fomenting prejudices against other species as well: Turkeys were mentally challenged. Foxes were sly. Bears were bumbling. Cats were coy.

Recalling the Metzgers' discussions of the dangers of prejudice, Kelev planned to file a complaint with Pittsburgh's Office of Animal Rights and had scheduled depositions with representative animals. He would pursue justice: that was G-d's wish.

At 8:00 a.m. the next morning, Kelev ducked out of his house for his first appointment. It was time to talk turkey. Tom, a wild turkey, wandered onto Kelev's lawn, and Kelev approached him.

"How are you doing?" Kelev asked.

"I am trying to squash the stereotype that turkeys are stupid. I squawk at the insults: turkey, bird brain— you know the slurs."

"Such fowl play. I bet those charges knock the stuffing out of you," Kelev said. "So, how do you demonstrate your intelligence?"

"I'm a mathematician. I attended MIT."

"What is MIT?" Kelev asked.

"Mathematics Institute for Turkeys."

"How much math do you know?"

"Test me."

"What is the circumference of a pumpkin?"

"The diameter times pi."

"Is pi like pumpkin pie?"

"Close enough."

"You're brilliant!" Kelev marveled.

"Thank you," Tom said. "Some people say my math is gobbledygook, but clearly you understand it."

The next witness, Freddy the fox, trotted over.

"Do you like the way I dance?" Freddy asked.

"I think you're fast on your feet," Kelev said.

"People allege I'm sneaky. That's not true," said Freddy.

"So what's your complaint?" Kelev asked.

"I can't find employment," Freddy said. "I have completed vocational training as a security guard. I am seeking a job guarding a hen house, but nobody will hire me. That's discrimination."

"What's the problem?" Kelev asked.

"The chickens are afraid of me."

"Maybe that's why they are called chickens," Kelev muttered. "But I've noted your complaint."

Next, Teddy the bear waddled onto the scene.

"People push me around. I have to hug little kids when they go to bed at night. I have to pose for makers of stuffed animals. And I have to fight forest fires."

"It sounds like you're being pulled in too many directions," Kelev observed.

"I'm battling stereotypes. People think I'm soft and cuddly. They say I sit on a log and eat honey all day."

"We have to tell people about the burdens you bear," Kelev said.

Kefira, the cat, showed up. "I know I have to give testimony, but I don't have much time. I'm due at a pedicure."

"You pamper your precious paws," Kelev said.

"You ask questions with dogged determination," Kefira replied.

"You're a perky little princess," Kelev giggled.

"So, I understand you're now a big macher in the animal rights community," Kefira said.

"Yes, I'm building bridges between animals and humans," Kelev said.

"I don't want to complain," Kefira said, "but ...."

"You don't need to complain. My cousin Kwetchie can take up the slack."

"People say cats are finicky. That's not quite true. I don't want cats to get a bad reputation."

"Then let's simply characterize cats as meticulous and discriminating."

"Much better," Kefira said. "Now, let's hope they don't bungle my pedicure."

Tomorrow, Kelev would compile his depositions into a report for the Office of Animal Rights. He needed to act soon, for he worried about the potential hatred that the Petless People Party might sow. He recalled Mr. and Mrs. Metzger's warning to their children about the dangers of an extremist group spewing hatred. But he felt confident that his report would offer compelling evidence of the animals' grievances and evoke public sympathy for them. It could even persuade Petless People Party members to become animal lovers. But all this thinking was exhausting. Having earned a nap, he stretched out on the kitchen floor.

12

...

The Sacred Scorecard

O nce again, Kelev was hard at work, unleashing his creative genius to help Jews connect with their faith.

Kelev's neighbor Kefira had not seen him for several days, but she had noticed Mrs. Metzger bringing bowls of dog food to the Metzgers' garage. Curiosity drove Kefira to poke her head into the garage where she found Kelev assembling a mind-boggling device consisting of a processing unit, a small screen, rubber tubes, and electrodes. It looked like an electrocardiogram machine.

"Hey, Kelev!" Kefira called out. "What are you making?"

"Don't bother me now. I'm busy," Kelev said gruffly.

"Please tell me," Kefira pleaded. "Perhaps I can help."

"Okay," Kelev said. "I'm almost finished developing the Yidometer."

"What does it do?"

"It tests one's fidelity to Judaism."

Kelev explained that the machine measured adherence to Judaism based on three dimensions: knowledge, charity, and spirit for Jewish life. The operator connected the Yidometer's electrodes to the subject's head, chest, and belly. The head electrode measured knowledge of Jewish prayers, rituals, laws, and history. The chest electrode monitored the heart, picking up commitment to charity (Tikkun Olam). The belly electrode peered into the soul. Kelev had included this electrode because he believed that the soul lay in the stomach. The soul gives every living being purpose and a connection to G-d, he reasoned. The soul sustains life, and what sustains life more than a meaty meal? The Yidometer would read the subject's knowledge, intentions, and commitment to Judaism, score each dimension, and then provide a composite score ranging from 1 to 100.

"What led you to invent this thing?" Kefira wanted to know.

"I'm a busy mitzvah macher for G-d. This device will help G-d decide who will be inscribed in the *Book of Life* each year."

"So, you help keep score for G-d?"

"Yes, like a yeshiva bocher keeping the books."

"How did you get this idea?"

"I drew inspiration from two Jewish dogs, Kichel and Kreplach, who run an accounting practice for dogs.

They crunch numbers to keep track of food inventories. So I figured I would invent a machine that crunches numbers for yiddishkeit."

"Let's test it!" Kefira suggested. She attached the three electrodes to Kelev. The device made a faint humming noise for two minutes, then flashed the results: a composite score of 98.6. Kelev was delighted.

"Wow!" Kefira exclaimed. "This machine seems to work. I thought it might blow up."

"Of course it works," Kelev said. "Let's try it on you."

He tested Kefira, who scored only 72. "This contraption says I have some work to do," she grumbled. "It does not measure my beauty, compassion, warmth, benevolence and charm."

"Sorry, Bubala. The numbers are the numbers."

"I wonder how I compare to our neighborhood friends?" Kefira asked.

"Let's do some field testing," Kelev said.

Like two kids selling lemonade, Kelev and Kefira set up a stand on the sidewalk and put the Yidometer on it. The testing clinic was now open. Schmalzie, Schmoozie, Borscht, Kwetchie, and other neighborhood dogs all came to be tested. Their scores ranged from 60 to 90. "Hmm," Kelev said, as he pored over the results. "Not bad, but certainly not perfect."

Kelev wasn't satisfied. He sought perfection. He put the machine in a carrying case and packed a doggy travel bag. "I'm off," he said.

"Where to?" Kefira asked.

"To find a Jew who achieves a perfect score."

"Dog, cat, or person?"

"It makes no difference," Kelev said grandly. "We are all made in G-d's image."

Whom would Kelev find, Kefira wondered—an angel, a prophet, or even the Messiah? Or would it be a Yiddishe mama with a flair for cooking? The thought of the Yidometer humbled Kefira, for she realized that it forced each subject to come to terms with the reality that he or she stood alone, in awe before the Creator.

Kefira returned home to embark on her own journey of learning. Memories of her grandparents inspired her to embrace her heritage. She anticipated a visit from Kelev, when she would "negotiate" with the Yidometer again.

13

...

Kefira Finds Faith

Kefira had always fluttered around like a social butterfly, but her frivolous flight was about to end. She faced the day of reckoning, when she would have to account for herself before her Creator. Had she been a good Jew? She fretted because her Yidometer score of 72 wasn't good enough. She wanted to improve her standing in G-d's eyes. Memories of her grandparents inspired her to embrace her Jewish heritage. She felt an emotional bond with Judaism because a Jewish family had adopted her grandparents from an animal shelter.

If this family had not intervened, Kefira's grandparents might have been put to rest much too young.

Kefira felt pressure to improve her Jewish knowledge and spirit soon, for she lived with the daily expectation that Kelev would show up to administer the test again. As the day of reckoning approached, the prospect of accounting for her life overwhelmed her. Previously she had believed that cats had nine lives. She realized now that every living being makes only one appearance on Earth. Unlike baseball, life has only one inning. And unlike baseball, life is not a game.

Fortunately her guardians, Leon and Ariela Katz, had always nurtured Jewish values: compassion for all living beings and respect for learning. Mr. and Mrs. Katz fed seeds to birds during the winter and provided shelter to stray cats. They kindled the light of learning. And lately, Kefira had hung around the dining room when the Katzes lit the Shabbos candles and discovered that being part of this ritual ignited a fire in her soul to illuminate Judaism. So the Katzes sent Kefira to a special school, the Kindergarten for Kosher Kittens, where she began studying the sacred text Mishna, Midrash, and Meows. Kefira also started participating in Pittsburgh's chapter of the National Council of Jewish Female Felines, and she joined the sisterhood in her shul, Beth Aryeh.

In addition to studying Hebrew, she learned some Yiddish and reveled in dropping Yiddishisms into her conversation.

"Why does Mrs. Katz kvetch when I come into the house with muddy paws?"

"I'm learning so much. The Gantseh Megillah!"

"Oy, I'm so verklempt when I think I might fail the Yidometer test."

Then one Friday morning, Kelev appeared in her backyard.

"So, you're here to administer the Yidometer?" Kefira stuttered. She was actually trembling; her heart pounded.

"No," Kelev said. "I threw it away."

"Why?"

"I realized that you can't reduce a living being's essence to a single number. That constitutes a judgment. Mortals can't judge other mortals—only G-d can judge."

"I thought G-d was going to use the Yidometer to determine who will be inscribed in the Book of Life each year."

"G-d is all-knowing. G-d doesn't need a fancy gadget."

"But then how can I tell whether I have been a good Jew and lived a righteous life?"

"Peer into your soul. Invoke the concept of Tikkun Olam. Have you tried to make the world a better place?"

So Kefira reflected on her life. She regretted her past sarcasms and frivolous pranks. She rejoiced in helping the tired, sick, hungry, and lost stray cats that her guardians welcomed. A sense of calm engulfed Kefira as she ushered in Shabbos with them. In a Jewish home, they would never be homeless.

14

...

Kelev Makes Aliyah

One day, Mrs. Metzger received a letter from her ninety-two-year-old great aunt, Anna Schwartz, who lived in Israel. Aunt Anna wrote that she had been reflecting on her life, during which she had requested only a few things from G-d. In 1943, Aunt Anna had asked G-d to spare her from the gas chambers during her captivity in Treblinka. Now, in 2016, she had another request: a companion to dispel loneliness during her final days. She had no more relatives in Israel, so Aunt Anna asked Mrs. Metzger for ideas about finding such a companion.

This letter touched Mrs. Metzger. She knew that Aunt Anna loved dogs because of their innocence. She believed that humans, with their unlimited capacity for evil, could learn from dogs.

It occurred to Mrs. Metzger that Aunt Anna would adore Kelev. The Jewish people had given the world the gift of humor. And Kelev was the ultimate version of that gift—for who in the world was funnier than Kelev?

During dinner that evening, Mrs. Metzger told her husband and children about Aunt Anna's letter and broached the idea that Kelev could make Aliyah to Israel to live with her. Mr. Metzger protested, "Kelev belongs to our family. How can we part with a family member?" Both parents and children began to cry.

Once they regained their composure, the oldest daughter, Naomi, asked, "Who will take Kelev on walks and help Aunt Anna take care of him?" Mrs. Metzger had thought of that. She responded that Israel had several social services agencies that helped the elderly and promised to consult their rabbi to find one.

Adam asked, "Who will take care of Kelev when Aunt Anna becomes a blessed memory?" Aliyah cements a sacred bond with G-d, his father told him. The family could not expect Kelev to return to Pittsburgh. Instead, Aunt Anna's passing would serve as G-d's invocation to

their family to make Aliyah to Israel to join Kelev. The prospect of Kelev's departure left Mr. Metzger and the children heartbroken. But they agreed that Kelev would bring Aunt Anna nachas.

After dinner, Mrs. Metzger saw Kelev lying under the dinner table. "I'm sure you heard our conversation," she said. Kelev looked sullen; a tear rolled down his face. "Please think about an Aliyah, my dear Kelev," Mrs. Metzger begged and began to cry again.

That evening, Kelev considered the prospect of joining Aunt Anna in Israel. He knew he would miss his family and friends in Pittsburgh. But he felt an obligation to comfort Aunt Anna. She was one of the few surviving members of European Jewry, a community that barely escaped annihilation. Bringing joy to Aunt Anna would constitute a mitzvah, an affirmation of Jewish life in defiance of past hatred. Kelev knew that he had begun his journey as a Jew in order to bring light to Jewish life. That clinched it. Kelev decided to make Aliyah.

The next morning, Mrs. Metzger anxiously observed Kelev under the table and saw that he exuded calm. In this way she knew he had decided to move to Israel. Later that morning, Kelev told Schmalzie about the plan. "This isn't a schmaltzy story," Schmalzie commented. "This sounds real."

Word traveled fast around the neighborhood. Around noon, a delegation of Kelev's friends arrived to wish him shalom. Sammy the squirrel, Schmalzie, Roderick, Borchst, Schmoozie, and Kefira gathered in his yard to say farewell. "Why the long faces?" Kelev asked. "You all look like you're sitting shivah."

Sammy thanked Kelev for mediating the peace among the squirrels. He praised Kelev for following Jewish values—the application of laws and reason—to achieve peace. Roderick recalled how Kelev had helped him discover his own Jewish roots. Schmalzie spoke proudly of how he had mentored Kelev, guiding him toward a Jewish life. Kefira expressed gratitude to Kelev for his patience and for pointing her toward spiritual fulfillment.

The entire Metzger family traveled to Israel to bring Kelev to Aunt Anna. She lived in an apartment complex for elderly residents in Tel Aviv. It was a simple place; Aunt Anna was used to living in sparse conditions. When they arrived, Kelev ran right over to Aunt Anna. She hugged him, and he licked her cheek. It was a wet, slobbery, doggy kiss. Aunt Anna laughed and asked, "Are you trying to tell me I need a bath?" Aunt Anna was small and spry, still very alert. Her bearing was calm; her eyes reflected peace. Kelev marveled that she could still embrace life after witnessing the horrors of her youth. Only one picture hung on the wall: a 1940 photo of Aunt Anna with her parents and her four siblings in their home in Lodz, Poland. Kelev could recognize Aunt Anna and her oldest sister Sophie, Mrs. Metzger's grandmother.

A young social worker, Michal, came to help Aunt Anna with daily chores and take Kelev on walks. Each

day, she brought Kelev and Aunt Anna into the apartment building's yard where Kelev honed his skills chasing butterflies. Aunt Anna laughed at his antics.

For most of the day, Aunt Anna rested. These long periods of quiet gave Kelev time to reflect. It was hard to be a Jew.

Judaism didn't allow Jews to coast through life. What was the purpose of living a Jewish life? He had learned that Jews bore two obligations. The first was Tikkun Olam, making the world a better place for future generations. The second was honoring the memories of the righteous souls who died in pursuit of a Jewish life. Persecution pervaded Jewish history. Jews had endured enslavement in Egypt, the destruction of the Temple, the Diaspora, the Crusades, the Spanish Inquisition, pogroms, the Holocaust, and modern-day terrorism. But Jewish martyrs had died for a purpose—to sustain Jewish ideals and traditions.

Kelev missed the Metzgers and his friends in Pittsburgh. But the knowledge that he was bringing nachas to a Jewish heroine heartened him. He felt that his quest for Jewishness had now borne fruit, for he had reached his destination in his journey as a Jew. He had found his faith and performed the ultimate mitzvah.

No, it is not easy being a Jew. But life is not easy. When we face our Creator, we must account for ourselves: Have we made the world a more enlightened and caring place?

Such intense introspection made Kelev weary. He fell asleep. He will sleep with the joy of knowing that he has infused Aunt Anna's life with light and laughter. He will sleep with both eyes closed. He will sleep in peace.

Acknowledgements

I commend the skilled and dedicated professionals who helped to create this book. Editor Stephanie Golden offered poignant suggestions to advance the plot, improve the flow and pose thought-provoking insights. Illustrator Ed Shems captured the essence of the characters and made them spring to life. Designer Judith Arisman blended the text and illustrations in a balanced and exquisite manner.

Made in the USA
Columbia, SC
18 October 2017